AROUND YOU

ABHAY RAMAGIRI

Contents

Preface

This is the story of Chandra Shekhar (Chandu). A 14-year-old curious but confused boy. In his puzzling teenage days, he faced such an incident in his life when his habits started imposing penalties on him, his reactions started questioning his actions, and when each of his steps started back-firing.

Did he standstill or surrender to his surroundings?
In that process did he win himself or ruin himself?
Come, join his journey to unwrap.

I

Let's start with Balraju, Balu is a 3rd standard kid from an international school and a neighboring friend of Chandu, who stays at Block no 201, he is the kind of kid who prefers watching the discovery channel over cartoons. It was a balmy Sunday. A special chicken curry, no homework, and an episode of "man vs wild" filled his noon with happies. It has been his day so far, but greedy Balu wanted to have a bang in the evening, he arranged a cricket match with Sidhu's team, A boy who stays next to their stree. It was all set for an exciting match between "Balu bulldozers" and "Sidhu safaris" (as they like to call their teams), 4:30 PM was the toss time. Boundaries are very simple only towards long ON & long OFF and when the ball crosses the first tyre of the MARUTHI car (which was parked out there) it is declared as a boundary. Without any further delay, he took his bat and when he was about to step down the stairs, the message "bring the ball Balu" kicked in his ears, then he returned home. He took a glimpse under the bed. Anyway, it's going to be at its regular place but intense BGM in his mind made that moment more difficult. Swiped off all the shelves in the hall, shuts the door, picked the floor mat up...At the same time praying god not to ruin this day. After 5 minutes of struggle, he found that spherical rubber in the same place where he had previously kept it. He Picked it up with a smirky smile and moved forward. Chandu was distracted by the pit-pat sound from the stairs. He noticed his buddy standing in the corridor but sir was busy with PUBG. "Chandu bro...!" Balu yelled with enthusiasm but he didn't get any response from his senior.

"Hey, Chandu!" called politely.

"How dare you to call me by name! Give respect to take it back. Go! Go..! First, comb your hair properly" chandu replied.

"Sorry! Sorry! Chandu brother! Ok tell me won't you get bored of playing PUBG. Why don't we club together for a match?" raised his proposal.

"What match?"

"Cricket match brother, you will have fun" Balu replied in a joyful accent.

"What? Cricket! With your lilliput gang and you are assuring fun! Wow, Balu!" Chandu gave an ironic look to Balu.

"Why bro? What's so interesting about PUBG? Shooting! Shooting! Nothing new!"

Chandu Exclaimed "What is interesting! You are a kid. You can't taste that essence. That thrill factor, I want such kind of thrill not your barbie doll cricket match. Go! Your lilliputs might be waiting for you" turned and continued his game.

"OK bro, don't get excited, calm down" replied Balu.

"What? Excited! He has gone mad" Drones.

"I am going bro, can I know the time?"

"it's 4:20 Balu"

"4:20!!" exclaimed.

"Yes! 4:20 is the time, of course, 420 resembles you but now it's really 4:20 PM"

"Wo! No! No! I mean..." Tried to persuade.

"Haa! Go, kiddy! You got the satire! Now just go and enjoy."

"You! Chandu idiot, I'll get you after the match" drones and moved from the corridor. Whereas Chandu changed his posture in the chair and carried away with his game.

Pace added to the game, he was completely involved in it. Meanwhile his mom, Keerthana came into the action. Just came in from the balcony, she was busy with her chaos. She had a plan to attend a bhajan in the temple and she is almost running out of time. In a hurry "hey! Chandu can you get me the comb I couldn't find it" Yelled.

"Hey! kill that rascal...!" these were uttered from Chandu as he was completely into it.

"Hey, Chandu! Look here" his mom yells again.

"What Maa? I am listening" he sickeningly replied.

"I know you are listening, but I need your attention Chandu", on other hand she keeps on searching and trying with her peak ability to reach the temple as soon as possible; It's been almost 2 minutes she didn't get any reflex action from chandu and he provoked like "Maa it will be there itself, try try until you get success". Finally, she has gone for it and found it. "I found it aaand...you get busier in playing..." Said Keerthana; but those words did not work on this game.

Keerthana knew that there was a lot more to handle and set right in the house in that quick session, she moved into the kitchen and started managing all the stuff; Meanwhile, with a ray of hope she once again ordered Chandu to search for her specs and as usual, he replied with laze; as she was already irritated with her household work, his ignorance added frustration to it. Instead of shouting, inspired by her household serials she made a plan. In that view she found her specs and moved into the bedroom; she was like "please Chandu could you get my specs...I have no time." Anyway, he thought to go for it; kept his mobile aside, and took a wide look over his site. Then he found mom's reflection in the mirror, he understood her plan, and without any further delay grabbed his mobile and continued the game. After a few minutes when mom asked about it he replied: "Maa once search keenly in your hands you'll get it." Mom was like "this idiot never come out of that trance" nodes.

Keerthana messed up with Chandu's careless behavior, she literally couldn't bear it and she was done with him; So this time she planned to disturb him by assigning as many works as possible. In that view, she went to the kitchen and kept the milk jar on the stove to boil; then came to him and said "Chandu you have to do this!"

"OK Maa!"

"what OK? Now I'm going to assign you some work. If you want to drink milk-have it or else OFF the stove after 10 to 12 minutes."

"It's okay Maa, I'll handle it." He doesn't even look at her.

"What will you handle?" crossed his statement.

"Ok Maa, I will OFF it. As of now, you go to the temple peacefully"

"I am almost done. Once call your aunt and tell her to move," she said and moved away from him.

"Mom you know! These neighboring building construction workers are too fast. Today, that sand-loaded truck is going to come and make a mess over here" he thought he could deviate her. Then mom said "yeah! that's true but what I asked you and what are you talking about? Do what I say!" she replied from the kitchen.

"Shit! Maaa, you are really..!" he mumbled and said I can't Maa, I am busy in the match.

"I thought you are at the home! Then where am I? In the battleground!?" mom shot her sarcasm.

"Maa, stop joking. Please leave me!"

"No way! Or else you have another option; join me and, we'll go to the temple."

"No way!" he declared his opinion in less than a second.

"Then call her! At least do it with my mobile. Hurry up! I don't have much time."

She was all set to make a move. Chandu thought the latter one was far better, then he somehow managed both the mobiles and took the response from his aunt and said "Mom, she is on the way, you are the one prolonging the time." after listening that words she couldn't stop her anger; came like a chasing tiger near him and asked him to repeat the words, then he was like "No..! Nothing Maa!"

"No! You said something!"

"I just repeated what aunt said." He didn't dare to give eye contact; then she pulled off the mobile from his hands, Whereas Chandu has no idea of how his second is going to be, He lost all hopes in his game and stood there helplessly. After 2 minutes she returned his mobile and said "You have to switch off the water motor after 30 minutes, I am not testing your IQ; so kept an alarm for it. Switch it off when you hear the Chandramukhi alarm music. Do this. Hope, you know very well what I'll do!"

With an innocent expression nodded his head. For a few seconds, he was struck by those words. That deadly warning petrified him; At the same time, he was happy about his game.

Keerthana went inside the bedroom and memorized her son's eccentric expression and drones "Did I really scare him?!, Hope this warning *makes him attentive" and came out with her handbag. She was all set to move. Meanwhile, Chandu started a new match; he noticed his mom and got off of his chair to send her off; Keethana was like"As you said, the loaded truck is going to come and its dusty particles gonna ruin our floor, so close all the doors."*

"What about windows?"

"Yeah! even that; don't fall into that trance. If you make any nuisance, I will cut off your pocket money...take care!" with a sweet caution left that place.

"Sure Maa! I'll take care, By the way when you'll be back?"

"I'll be back at 7 PM" replied from the stairs.

Chandu came inside, closed the entrance door, took a comfortable seat, and continued his game without further disturbance. The game reached its peak moment, he was completely into it. It's been more than 10 minutes and 3 more kills to go; there comes the battery remainder. It reached 3%, as of his habit he took a look all around him for a charger without moving his body a single inch. When he was about to move from his position his friends started yelling at the speaker. He left the battery part and again carried away with the game. He was almost done, then came the notification of 1%; tension occupied his brain, he was carrying his mobile with his right hand and searching for the charger with the other hand. He couldn't manage both things. First, he switched on all the switches and just roamed various places in the house without a plan. He was repeatedly searching the same areas; in such a moment, he pulled off books from their shelves; some of these books pulled out the oil bottle which was placed behind them and it started flowing right away. He paused for a second after seeing it but he again ran for his cause of quest; nothing could make him happy. On the other hand, he started asking "bro...! What happened? Hey, respond guys! I am almost done. I'll go for the last kill. WINNER WINNER...."

"Hey...", there is no response. His realization was too late, His battery was dead. Now 70% of his brain came back to the practical world; he has no interest in searching for chargers. The very next idea that stuck in his mind is to ask Pithambaram Uncle for the charger. Pithambaram is a typical 55 years old miser who stays in the opposite flat 102.

Chandu was frustrated about that piece of wire. He knew that it was not that easy to convince Pithambaram, but his main intention was to have fun with uncle's typical mindset and weird accent. As he was messed up with that room and stuff; went to the balcony to embrace the pleasant air. There he noticed Balu and his team having a blast in the street and started moving towards Pithambaram's door with a positive urge.

5:15 PM

With a cunning smile, Chandu knocked on the door. As usual, 5 minutes later, he opened the door and returned to his bedroom.
"Uncle I'm here," Chandu yelled from the entrance. Pithambaram recognized the voice but again replied "who the hell are you?"
"What! Who the hell..! Idiot! How can he say that?" mumbled.
This time Pithambaram came out of his room and when he was about to say "who is..." he then pretended to see Chandu and took his words back.
Chandu: It's me, uncle.
Pithambaram: Oh! Sorry, Chandu! I'm extremely sorry. I thought some salesman had come.
Chandu wanted to say "Enough! Keep your non-funny jokes with you. Don't act too smart" But said"It's okay uncle! Never mind."
Pithambaram: That's ok, basically I won't get to see you, you are a busy person right! You are a determined PUBG player. Ok, tell me for what you have come?
Chandu: Will you reduce your satire size uncle! I couldn't bear it.
Pithambaram: Ok fine! As your wish, what do you want?
"Actually, I came to charge..."
Pithambaram interrupted him and asked "Chandu, casually asking you have written some exams right! What's your percentage? "
Chandu (mumbled): shit..! He started again..!
Pithambaram: Tell Chandu! You have to answer this. You are allowed to share those beautiful moments with me.
He wanted to ask "from which planet did you come, uncle? Can you share your experience?"But hesitatingly replied "Nothing to say, uncle! My percentage was okayish good"

Pithambaram: Oh! Written well?! Really, but I heard you just passed with an average mark.

Chandu was like "Thank god! Maa didn't reveal about that failed subject" and said "Ok uncle! Somewhat good."

Pithambaram: What about Mathematics and physical science?

Chandu: Yeah! I was the highest scorer in physical science.

Pithambaram: Ok! Ok! It happens! I strongly believe that these marks and ranks will define one's ability, intelligence, and sometimes character.

"Stop your nonsense, you idiot" drones Chandu.

Pithambaram: You were saying something! What do you want?

Chandu: Yeah! tell me, uncle! That was your responsibility to fix up the water motor switchboard right?

Pithambaram (jerks): It...Is...how!!

"Now tell me you! Even I can make you feel awkward. How can you imagine me being dumb!" drones Chandu.

Pithambaram: I...I will work on it...

Chandu: Hurry up, uncle! I'm not the one to tell you, but it is a biggie. By any little touch, it can be switched on, and when lenience comes into the action water may flow down through the stairs, if anyone steps on the watery floor, you know!

Chandu's narration showed a mini horror film to Pithambaram. For a second he got scared and said "yeah! I will! You were asking something about the charger, continue!"

"You, comedy piece! I know how to handle you" Chandu mumbled.

Pithambaram: What? Is that about the mobile charger?

Chandu: Yes uncle, I want to borrow your mobile charger for a few hours.

Pithambaram: I don't know! The extra piece might be damaged, I have to search for another one.

Chandu literally wanted to say "you bloody miser; what stops you to give me your charger; Does it cost anything?!" But controlled his agony and said, "Nothing wrong with it, uncle; take your time, or I can manage with your charger."

Pithambaram came up with an old micro-USB charger and again tried to manipulate him by connecting the USB wire in the wrong direction.

Chandu: uncle, you are doing it wrong. Let me fix it.

Pithambaram: By the way, what's the purpose to charge your mobile, Is it for PUBG?

Chandu: No...I mean...(mumbled in denial)

Pithambaram: No, I could sense it.

Chandu: Not at all, actually mom went to the temple and I need to respond to her if she calls, that's the reason I was asking for a charger, that's it.

Pithambaram: Ok fine. Take it.

After Successfully keeping his mobile on charge, with a satisfactory feeling he quietly and quickly returned to his home. Now Chandu has to spend at least 30 minutes without his mobile. He knew that it is going to be horrible to stay at home, without any gadgets and at that moment nothing could hold his interest to stay there; so he again picked up the lock and changed his direction. When he was about to open the door his mom's words knocked on his mind "Idiot! Close all the doors.". After shutting down all the doors and other windows, he felt like now he is eligible to lock the entrance door. Locked and cross-checked it. On the last count, he took an overview of his house. He found a zero bulb was glowing on the top of their entrance but he was like "It might be switched on while searching for a charger, whatever! Let it glow." Without any basic plan, he started moving down; slowly reached to the ground floor, switched off the motor; with a calm and relaxed mood started walking on the street. There is Balu, playing cricket with his friends. Chandu was exactly walking away from him. Balu was on the strike at that moment, and as he saw Chandu was walking, A creepy thought bounced in his mind, It was to hit a straight drive on Chandu's head. But, Chandu didn't even consider Balu's presence; His eyes were only on his way. Suddenly, A 5-year girl grabbed his attention; not even blinking his eyes. Watching her intensely. Whereas Balu raised his arms to smash the ball. Bowler came with a racing speed and bowled right under his legs. That's enough, he smashed an extra drive over the long-off but Chandu ran towards the girl and pulled her off from meeting up with an accident. Meanwhile, Balu's phenomenal drive kicked him into danger. Ball made a fancy tattoo on the window glass; which was more than enough to ruin his day. All the lilliputs reached their safe paths, with disappointment, Balu wrapped up his stuff and ran away.

Chandu is a savior now. Her father, who was smoking at a general store threw his gold flake(cigarette) down, rushed towards his daughter, and took her into his arms. The very next thing he did was to start praising the savior, and Chandu became as tall as their 3 floors building after digesting them. He thought to scold that big man for his negligence but he was carried away by those overwhelming words and he just replied "It's okay uncle, take care of her". There he noticed gentle eyes staring at him; it was none other than his uncle. Sudharshanam, A middle-aged courteous man left out with a general store. Chandu grins and started walking toward him.

Chandu: Uncle, can I get a cigarette?

Sudharshanam (smirked): Of course, we have various packs; would you like to take a jumbo pack?

Chandu with a sneaky smile said "No uncle. I want something bigger than that."

"Yeah! You can have it...only when you pay all your properties to me." replied Sudharshanam, then both laughed at their sarcastic words, and Chandu was like "Then how can you sell it to him!?

"He was just my customer. Ok, tell me, How did you manage that? It was so close. That car would have dashed you."

"Uncle, I couldn't freeze myself to do that. Life is not a cup of tea for me, I've just gone for it."

"But never go for such risky moves again, be conscious about your life too" Sudharshanam warned.

"It doesn't matter! I don't know why but I felt like it was my primary task," said Chandu.

"Ok, but be selfish."

"Sure uncle! Give me a green lays packet; see there it is." Took out 20 rupees and kept them on the table. Sudharshanam refused it and said, "Instead tell me, what was your percentage?" As Chandu was messed up with this dialogue, he gave that lays packet back and said "Keep it with you uncle, I am going. God bless you."

"Hey! Hey! What happened?"convinced him to stay back and Chandu

was like "Marks! Percentage! Marks! Percentage! Are you guys planning to prepare my resume?!"

"Nothing! I was casually asking."

"Ok! Ok! That's fine." Comparing his uncle with Pithambaram.

"Ha! Listen here, don't reveal any of your marks but all I can say is just defeat your previous version every day, That's enough! Anyhow, we cannot judge the kids of this generation by their marks" Chunked.

"Oh! Well said, uncle. Definitely," Stricken the words 'comparing them both'.

Sudharshanam stared at Chandu and said "One more thing! The moment when you stop doing this you will get a free membership premium."

"Free membership? Free membership for what?" Chandu asked confusingly.

"A free membership to join in Idiots Club." Loudly laughed.

"Sudharshan uncle! You are literally..."

Sudharshanam: But I'm sure that club members won't accept you.

Chandu: Thank god! You know me. I am not the one who gives up.

Sudharshanam: Let's see. Hope for the best. By the way, what's your favorite subject?

Chandu: Physics is a crazy subject right! I started loving it in the past few months but the problem is, mom is ceasing me from performing experiments at home premises. I don't know how but you have to convince her and she should allow me.

Sudharshanam knocked his head for a minute and said "Ok fine! I will definitely convince your mom but on one condition!"

"What is that?" he asked hesitatingly.

"The condition is you should never keep any bomb under my shop. I am a poor bugger."

"Definitely not! If I place it who will give me a free lays packet" chunks.

"You idiot..........!" exclaimed Sudharshanam. When they are having great fun; all of a sudden a customer hurriedly came and interrupted them, ordered a milk packet, and when Sudharshan gave him the product and asked for money his face turned black. After a period of struggle somehow, he convinced Sudharshanam and finally managed to take a

500ml milk packet with him. Whereas Chandu was stunned by seeing this and started shouting "Uncle, this is ridiculous! How can you credit him a product like that? I mean why!?"

"Chandu, you know this business only runs on a good trust and belief system" smoothly replied.

"How can you believe him?" he asked with a puzzling face.

"The only rule I know is if you believe in yourself; you will know whom to believe. Your soul never suggests you a wrong path and I'm pretty sure he will return my money any day."

"So believing is important! That's it!"

"Yes! Chandu."

"Ok!" Chandu started reasoning that statement and Sudharshanam said, "But the thing is that was the only milk product left; your aunty said to bring one while returning."

"What product?!" hesitatingly

"Milk! Why?"

"oh my god!! Milk packet... home! Holy shit" he mumbled and said," I should go uncle; I'll be back after some time."

Like Mahesh in the movie POKIRI, Chandu rushed back with his peak ability all over from the general store. Even that intense BGM(background music) was playing in his mind. He pushed off their gate with anger; slipped on the stairs a couple of times but managed to reach their corridor, he then picked up the lock, another hand went to his pocket and his face turned pale; he started screaming "Key! Man....!" There comes the biggest task for him. He had gone out of his senses. His mind appeals to search in other pockets but his body was just listening to the words of tense. Ignoring the word logic, he started searching on the floor, and wall. For every 2 seconds looking at the angry face of the lock and making hell out there. His mom was dancing on his head; her words kept on multiplying his tension and killing his intelligence. Speed of light was nothing compared to his flow of negative thoughts; for a second, locked himself and took a position; touched his right and left pocket with a little hesitation. Again he could sense nothing. His agony reached the sky. He couldn't handle that situation, degrading himself. Thrown all the wet clothes which were hanging there. Pulled out the shoe case all the shoes fell out of its den, still, that couldn't satisfy his anger. Now his legs came into the action showing them a new destination in all directions. Screaming, striving to get rid of his stereo drama, All of a sudden there was a little spark in his eyes; as he found something lustrous in the corner of the shoe case. Without any further delay, he bent for it, but again he stepped on shit. It was a 1-rupee coin. That spark in his eyes turned out to be a conflagration, his patient molecules evaporated. A barbarous creature came out of him, with all his power elevated the shoe case and threw it towards the stairs; after a couple of turns, it gave a high-five to the water motor board.

Balu, the window smasher, secretly watching this chaos for the past 5 minutes. There was a mixed emotion flowing in him; strengthening himself to join the confusion and when he noticed Chandu was going beyond his senses, he couldn't stop himself to control that man, with a little courage, moved towards him, grabbed Chandu's hand and somehow managed to make him sit.

"Cool brother! Cool! You just relax, let me bring you some water. Please don't move." said Balu.

He bought water in a red bottle. Chandu picks up the bottle and gulped heavily.

Balu: Now tell me, bro! What has actually happened? Why you have messed up things like this?

Chandu: What? Who messed up?! I was in a dilemma and went with the flow.

Balu: Ok! You got tensed, but why?

In a softer tone replied "Hey it's nothing! It was mom's strict order to off the stove and because of this bloody key.....!"

Balu: It was a small mistake. Later you can apologize to her bro. First, you calm down!

Chandu: She was so serious about this. But that's not the matter, she said she's gonna cut my pocket money.

Balu: oh! This is bigger! If not (thod dhen-gey). Let's break the lock.

Chandu with a sarcastic look "WOW! What an idea! You are a genius Balu"

Balu: Mention not brother!

Chandu: You idiot!! For a 20 rupees milk product, no one will break the 100-rupees lock. Now if we break this lock, Mom won't take any time to break my head.

Balu: Sorry! Sorry! Then what should we do now?

Chandu: Wait for a second! Milk is on the stove, right? It would be burnt out, but there is no smell. Thankgod gas might be completed in the cylinder.

Balu: Yeah! Yeah! That's true, but I could sense some other smell.

Chandu changed his posture. Shifted to a relaxed mood. He was like "Just leave it! It! Listen here, One thing I learned from this situation. We should not get tensed man! Being calm is important."

Balu: Yes! Yes! Got it, sir..!!

Chandu: Enough! See how hypertension killed my intelligence.

Balu (mumbled): This is realization!!!

Chandu: "PAST IS PAST GONE IS GONE", we have to be as accurate as possible from this moment.

Balu: Wow quotations! By the way, what happened to our beloved Pithu(Pithambaram)? You were making hell out here and there is no reaction. Strange!

Chandu: He is really strange! No matter what time is, he just sticks to his bed or else gives unnecessary suggestions. Here I should thank you, man! You made me calm.

Balu was happy about those words but deep inside he was nervous about his mistake and then hesitatingly said "But I have an apology for you."

Chandu: For what buddy!

Balu: I had broken your kitchen window glass. You have to manage aunt from scolding me and if possible throw my ball back.

Chandu felt something fishy, his focus was on the smell. "What?! You are still asking for the ball, pray to god! But that's not the point, can you smell something?" hesitatingly asked.

Balu: What bro? Smell! I already mentioned it.

Chandu: You idiot! Gas started leaking in my house, why didn't you inform me about this before?

Confused Balu "but how! What did I do?"

Chandu: Idiot! Your bloody match. Your ball did this.

Balu: You mean...milk was hit by me? I mean my ball!

"Yes! That milk fell on the stove, and the flame was gone! This is ridiculous man!"Exclaimed Chandu and stood up.

Balu has gone out of his senses. Again Chandu was like "Lot more to do! All lives are in our hands now, we have no time; if not boom! This building will collapse. Moreover, this is the 1ˢᵗ floor." Not his building but Balu]collapsed after listening to it. Chandu picked him up and both started searching for the key; again the same searching scenario but another donkey was added to the frame. This time Balu came up with an idea "Bro! First, we have to close Pithu's door if not he will..."

Chandu: what?!

Balu: Let's do this. Nothing will happen.

Chandu apparently agreed to that statement. His hands were searching for keys but he was completely obsessed with his past actions and negative thoughts, he was trying to analyze the situations but nothing seems to be working. All of a sudden a thought raised his head towards the door, there was a bulb glowing while he was moving out but now it wasn't glowing, and that helped his heart to reduce its volume.

Chandu: hey Balu idiot! Look at there, that bulb isn't glowing which means there is no power in his area.

Balu: Yeah! So what?

Chandu: That means, there is no electric supply around us. So we have some more time to get the key, you better manage something here, let me go downstairs. I'll search there.

Balu: Ok! Good luck brother! I'll manage.

This time Chandu was very conscious; as he opened the gate, two 6-feet raged workers crossed him with an 8-feet bed. This made him feel more guilty about his mistake, and he was like "What the worst fate is written to these new 3ʳᵈ-floor tenants, how to convey to them that they are heading towards their coffin. What mistake did these workers make to leave their lives here." Without pulling anyone's attention he started searching every corner of the road and reached the tip of street. Sudharshan noticed Chandu's tension, but he was quite busy with his customers. Whereas Chandu was drained with confusion. No matter what, he finished the work and quickly returned to the main gate.

There comes another check to his game. It was a fully loaded sand truck parked right under their building. Another contradiction in his moves, with various reasons more and more people were gathering there which was encumbering him. Workers were all set to unload the truck but they were tagged by one of their co-workers who was eating; when it comes to Chandu, he was in a trance of regret, his thought process was like "Key! Key! This bloody tiny metal piece is causing these many deaths. Why these many people should pay their lives for my mistake.!" And at the same time, his shade-2 was like "Leave it! Let them lead their karma. We should have nothing to regret. In the world of uncertainty, we cannot find even a single authentic soul. Who knows these workers might have a plan to kill someone, and even who knows 3rd-floor tenants might have evil thoughts. Anyhow Pithambaram deserves this; we are living in a lake full of crocodiles man! Let them suffer." He didn't get convinced by his shade-2 but was tackled by the dilemma. His senses were directing him to leak the news and also to appeal for help, but he was afraid of people like Pithambaram who prefers to raise their voice rather than their plan. Always ready to give free advice, scoldings, and mess the area instead of taking part for good cause. As he was thinking about the impurities of the world, he gained some self-confidence, ignored all his thoughts, and pushed himself to pull the gate.

*6:15 PM

When he was going across the path he took a glimpse over the parking area. There he noticed the shoe case in a corner that was thrown by him. With a little hope reached the corridor. Balu, who was waiting to execute something, ran towards him. "Bro! It's been more than 5 minutes. We should not hold on to it. Did you get the key? Let's open the door." said. Frustrated Chandu "Exactly I was about to ask you. What the hell you were doing till now."
Balu: I was searching and at the same time thought about PLAN-B. Wait...!Ush...! They are coming, let's move aside.
The same two workers going up carrying a refrigerator this time. "Shit! Bloody interruptions," mumbled Chandu.

Balu: In fact, look at there, the bulb is glowing now, the power came just before a minute. Now even god left us alone.

Chandu: damn! For the god's sake propose your PLAN-B!!

Balu with a little smile "We had killed a lot of time, even 3rd-floor tenets visited their house. He has seen me, so let's break the lock."

"Yeah! You are right! 100/- lock isn't a big deal in front of our lives. Cool! Let's do this!" Chandu controlled himself.

"Yeah! That's true!" said Balu.

"Closing all the doors and windows of our house saved us till now, but before it backfires we should break the lock."

Balu: Come on get a stone. Run! Run!

Both started the race targetting their street. When they were about to cross the parking area they noticed a child worker coming up carrying kitchen appliances, and there was a "kipiq mortor[rokali]" in them which was more than enough at that instant. Chandu caught him and convinced him to further proceedings. As soon as he got that, they rushed to the spot with a blend of happiness and nervousness. Gave a single tight slap on the lock, and its bang caused a mini disruption through 10 meters radius. No matter what they did their job. Two gratifying postures entered the house one after another. Little hesitatingly Balu asked, "Bro wait! Do you have a back pocket?"

Chandu: Of course I have! These are cargo shorts. You idiot is this the question to ask now!

Balu: Sorry! But is there any chance of key sleeping in it?

With an annoying expression, Chandu checked his pocket; unfortunately, he found it. Gave a pathetic look to Balu and said "Stop concentrating on my ass. You unlock the Pithambaram door first." He has no time to regret it, whisked into the kitchen and switched off the stove. Meanwhile, Balu was back, switched off all the switches, quickly moved to the bedroom, and opened the windows. The oil that he previously threw goes on flowed and reached the balcony door, considering it Chandu attentively opened the door and jumped into the balcony.

Took a deep breath, he could sense the cool breeze swings pulling out his sweat vapors. Ecstasy was just a word, he turned around and took the support of the balustrade- raised his head and had a wide look over the street. His eyes were embracing the existence of his street, just enjoying the desi chaos, and mumbled "Yes! I did it! All done! Let's apologize mom; let her scold me; I deserve it. But this moment.....! I'm with me that's enough."

Bonny sunset, soothing music in his head was making that moment more special. The idea that he saved the street gave him rapid goosebumps. For a second closed his eyes and suddenly busted out "Yes!!! Chandu you did it, man! Yes! this is really...! Man...shit! why I'm not getting any words?! Who cares, this happiness is enough." But in all these rush of thoughts a little snail-sized hesitation gliding in him that something is going wrong. It couldn't manage to survive in his peak vibe and he was like "never mind; let's enjoy this moment." After 2 minutes, he picked out the key from his back pocket, his eyes couldn't bear that metal piece, so he moved two 2 steps back, tied his anger to it, and threw it with his complete strength. Elevated his arms, and wanted to shout "Yahoo!" but the so-called insecurity stopped him but it failed to stop his mind to flush dopamine.

When he was flowing in the ocean of joy, chandramukhi's song started playing in their adjacent flat. Something struck his mind, meanwhile, Balu was washing his face. It's been a tough session for a 9-year kid. He was done with the day, whereas Chandu started digging into his thoughts; he turned around and commanded Balu to stop the tap. Silence occupied the place. Balu followed the order but he felt odd with Chandu's tone, so started moving toward the balcony. Chandu got to hear a noise from his right, there was an exterior plumbing pipe extending from the water tank. He placed his right ear exactly beside the pipe, as he was tallying his past with the present he found his mistake; his hesitation didn't go wrong. His eyes turned red, he was out of control, and his future was flashing in his eyes on a black frame; pointed his hand toward Balu and screamed "Holyshit! Hey, balarajuuu our water motor was switched on man! Look at here, listen to the flow of water, It's rushing from the terrace. This gonna ruin my life. That bloody shoe case. A mini pond might be formed there but that's not a big deal......workers are going......." Balu couldn't take it. He ran toward the balcony to hear, to recheck it. Chandu was screaming "No! careful.....oil..!" But as expected he was again tackled by his own mistake. Balu stepped on the oil and after a crazy dance moment in the air straight away fell on the legs of Chandu. BANG!!

As Balu has fallen on Chandu's legs. Chandu has gone out of control and followed the gravity. Flying! Flying! Flying! and utterly landed on the sand- the sand truck which was placed right under their building. He never thought that this Building construction work would save him. Not even a single person on the street noticed this 5-seconds drama. No one came to lift him. Meanwhile, Balu's little brain gave up on that situation, he fainted there itself.

THE DRAMA BEGINS *[6:30 PM]*

This landing was nothing less than a cinematic drama; his situation was so tangled, willing to thank god for a safe landing but at the same time want to scold him for making his next hours worst. Now his self-esteem reached 'O', confidence levels 'O' and Intelligence to '-1'. His mistakes one after another flashed in his eyes; then there comes the **'Nasty negativity'** *- The black part of every human brain. Freshly entered into Chandu's life and now popped out from his brain. Took a comfortable seat on his hair.*

It started its ferocious speech.

First of all, I would like to thank Mr. Chandra Shekhar for allowing me to ruin his life, sorry it's already ruined right!? You know, my worst master! If anyone tells you that they admire you or you are the best or nothing is impossible, just give them a tight slap with your left shoe.

Yes! You are No.1, in the batch of worst.

What can we do rather than sleep like a loser on this sand! Ok let's start an organization (WSO) World's shameless organization; obviously, you will be the president and my support will always be there for you. We were born to achieve it right!

Chandu couldn't able to control his 'Nasty negativity' (his negative thoughts). His soul wanted to say "I am not that worst" to himself but nothing was in his control. His 'Nasty negativity' was like "The statement should be like 'Nothing is possible' because we are the brand ambassador of hypertension hub right.! What? What? What? You are a *pro PUBG player, right? Is that worthy? We were searching like a dog for a mobile charger about it. Instead, you have thrown the oil bottle and now experiencing its fabulous result. How is this sand treatment, my boss!? Enjoying! We will definitely be recognized as one of the greatest idiots in the world, and you deserve it. Hypertension, anxiety, laziness. We should be proud of these habits. Now! Just Now! You have seen that the shoe case was kept aside but, what you did? you just ignored it. But still, I love you. You are my hero because you are my godfather. Anyhow water flow won't take much time to reach the 3rd-floor. If workers with their huge appliances step on the watery stairs, they gonna roll over and over and over on the stairs and die. Then you will be the primary suspect in their death and you will be cherished in the history of stupidity. My useless king! So anyhow we have taken the membership of the idiots club, I have a plan for you; instead of becoming a ball in a mom vs destiny football match let's pretend to be fractured. Let's use this sympathy card. Chandu's brain was infected with these thoughts. He was criticizing, degrading, and demotivating himself. The morals that he sought from his parents were not letting him get convinced to plan. This dissatisfaction with his negative side added fuel to a nut-size positivity in him. For the first time, he felt happy about his dilemma and inconvenience. Ignoring all the external struggles he wanted to rectify his mistake, he wanted to restrict the workers but he couldn't move. All he needed was a little push. But again the 'Nasty negativity' entered "Hey! Hold on! hold on! What! Do you want to save the workers? Wow! Do you think that you were born to save the world? You are not a savior!"*

'Positive Paramatma' *joined the show "Yes! He is a savior. Why should he sit still? He has enough capability to handle this situation. He is nothing less than others. In fact, he has extra baggage and that's you. You are the reason for his sadness."*

Nasty negativity: See, here comes the superstar, philosopher. Don't ever try to teach me.

Positive Paramatma: Yes! I'm nothing less than a superstar. I'll always be there for a boy like Chandu; why should he wait for the world to encourage him! You are the reason for Chandu's anxiety and now you are blaming him for that. I will never let him down, I am here to kill you!!!

Nasty negativity: I am his black version, I'm his shadow; you can't even touch me.

Chandu was deprived of these thoughts. His heart was sobbing with eternal perplexity. He wanted to go with a positive urge and put an end to this quest but the words and dark humor that he formally heard from his relatives and neighbors became weapons to Nasty negativity. Subconsciously he knew that he was overthinking and allowing negativity to rule his brain but these words were adding more and more fuel to pull himself down.

Nasty negativity: My idea is very simple. For useless people like us, this is the best choice, no risk, moreover who cares about water wastage and humans life. This sympathy card is more than enough. Let's enjoy the mood of laziness.

Positive Paramatma: We are never late to work for a good cause. Who gave us the right to kill someone just with our negligence? This is totally unfair man!

Nasty negativity: In the world of uncertainty who are.....

Positive Paramatma: Yes, the world is uncertain but that should not drive you to break your ethics. Let's create our own path rather than following the plural.

Yes! We were lazy and we were tense. Let's thank god for showing us heavy consequences for our mistakes, Yes! We got led down by Balu's mistakes too, instead of blaming him let's thank him. We might get scoldings from mom, and we might miss our pocket money but we got a lot to seek from these situations, we will never get to experience this emotional roller coaster again. Let's be glad for this drama and let's be glad to get scolded by mom.

Come on Chandu! Let's do this, give it a try, who cares about the result.! We are born to chase man! Till now, we had only experienced the joy of killing(virtually), now let's embrace the happiness of saving people. Man, It all depends on how we gonna deal with this situation. Let's make the right decision at this right moment.

Nasty negativity: Nothing is possible my mate.

Positive Paramatma: You can't do anything now, he is no more yours Mr.

nasty negativity; justified your name.

Try Chandu! Try! Just ignore the words of negativity. As our physics sir said we have good sensibilities on the practical knowledge, let's prove it once again. We were lacking in believing in ourselves as Sudharshanam said let's replace confusion with confidence we can do anything Chandu.! Chandu gave a jerk. "Come on, Champ. Let's do this." Positive Paramatma cheered. That words of Sudharshanam pumped him. Nasty negativity turned into negligible negativity.

**6: 43PM*

Chandu gets down from the truck with tons of positive urge. His posture was portraying his notion, without any second thought he gave a furious kick to the gate and ran into the building. All the workers in construction were astonished by his motion. Workers tried to interrogate him but no one could match his speed. He quickly reached halfway down the stairs and switched off the motor. Half burden carried out from him; continued his run towards his target. Deep inside praying to God for all good. All of a sudden a pit-pat sound(footsteps) struck his ears; it was from upstairs even his heart started replicating that footsteps sound. No matter what he reached his block. The overview of his house was like a bowl full of vegetable peels; when he was about to move that footsteps reached him, it was the new tenant guy rushing from the top floor. Both Chandu and the tenant guy were confounded by seeing each other. He was none other than the smoking guy.

"What are you...I mean....!" smoking guy was in a haste to go down.

Chandu: what?

Smoking guy: I mean, why? What are you doing here?

"This is my....." he was about to complete his words but the smoking guy started saying "I am so sorry buddy, but I have to go. I need to off the water motor switch. Construction workers are idiots! They don't even know how to construct a terrace, look at their water was flowing and it almost reached the 2-floor! Ridiculous!"

Chandu: Uncle I have two things to tell you. You just chill! It was done. I switched it off and just increase your volume and continue scolding them.

Smoking guy: You are really a savior man! How can you be at the right

place at a right time? First that car thing and now. No words.
Chandu: Actually....uncle...!
Smoking guy: Don't embarrass me am just 30; call me Raman.
Chandu: Fine brother! Actually, it was my mistake. It all started with Pithanbaram uncle, he stays in 102. He was the one who broke this motor switch and one of my foolish things made this.
Raman: oh! It happens, but don't repeat okay! By the way, there was a shoe case. Is that your?
"He caught the point" Chandu mumbled and said "Yeah! Yeah!" But underlyingly a query was hunting him. He knew he was not done yet, so hesitantly asked "I have a doubt! As you know heavy loads were been shifted till now, did workers face any trouble while moving on these watery steps."
"Yes! You guessed it right. A worker was about to slip" replied Raman. Chandu was seeled. "But again my daughter Appu. She made things normal; when workers were coming she indicated them to come slowly and later they informed me and there you go. I am here."
"Thank god! That means I saved myself!" droned Chandu.
"What's going on Chandu? What are you doing here?" keerthana yelled from the stairs, annoying atmosphere around her made her angrier.
Raman: Hello, aunty!
Keerthana: Hello....!!
Raman: I am Raman; from the 3rd floor.
Keerthana: oh..that new tenant guy. How are you? What about your new house?
Raman: I'm fine and the portion was good enough. So, where were.....?!
Keerthana: By the way, Chandu! What you have done? Is this the way you maintain a house?
"Daddy! Where were you?" Raman's daughter Appu came down the stairs with curiosity. Meanwhile, Chandu was happy about being skipped. Raman took her into his arms and said "Aunty! You know, Your son saved my daughter from meeting up with an accident; just an hour ago. You raised a savior aunty.! Thank you very much.!
Keerthana was overwhelmed by these words. Even Chandu thanked him for sharing this incident with his mom and said, "I just gave my best,

any way thankyou."

Keerthana: You made my day Chandu!

Raman: Even mine, keep raising Champ!

Keerthana: That's ok but What happened here Chandu? Who did this?

When Chandu was stammering to give a reply Balu entered the screen and said "Chandu bro! All fine, I have cleaned up the milk and I'm taking my ball back."

Keerthana: You Balarajuuu! What? What? What did you just say?

Chandu didn't want to hide his mistakes, "Let me tell you, Maa! Actually, there were multiple reasons. A few minutes ago I was in a hurry to search for the key and in that flow, I made this and I am very sorry about this Maa; the other one was Balu and his ball. He was the man behind this great chaos.

Keerthana: What!? This should be your last mistake, don't repeat it; and you Balu, stay tuned.

After listening to this; Chandu thought "Ahaa! God, you are great! Thank you so much for giving me this last chance. This is enough." and said, "Ok Maa! Thanks a lot for forgiving me, I won't repeat it."

All of a sudden Pithambaram opened the door and entered the corridor "Hey! What the hell is going on here!?"

Keerthana: Nothing! Did we disturb you, uncle!?

Pithambaram (grinned): No! No! Not at all. I was just asking what you all were doing here?

Keerthana: Ok! That's fine.

Pithambaram: When did you return from the temple?

Keerthana: Just now.

Pithambaram: By the way, What is this? Corridor or dump yard! Who did this? Where is that idiot!?

Chandu (mumbled): Shit! again...!?

Raman: Hello uncle! I am Raman, from the 3rd floor...

Pithambaram: Hello! Hello! You are a new tenant, right?

Raman: Yeah! Actually, these all happened because of you, uncle. I heard that you didn't repair the motor board switch and the rest is history, Water was flowing down and reached the 2nd floor.

Pithambaram face blushed with embarrassment. He couldn't bear it in front of his co-tenets. Raman secretly showed his thumb and winked at Chandu, and Chandu the happy man Enjoyed all the smiles around him and thanked God for struggling him. Finally, when he was about to enter into his house, he heard a battery-full notification from his mobile. He felt happy for not taking its help to solve his snags.

Here on, Chandu reframed his ideology that he can solve his problems on his own even without any gadgets, and patted himself by giving a smirky smile to his mobile.

"HE STARTED BELIEVING HIMSELF"
"NEVER LED HIMSELF DOWN"

ACKNOWLEDGEMENT

I feel so glad and excited to pen some names of whom I had a Great time with.

The two strong pillars of my story are my parents. Mrs. shailaja- my mother's ideologies always had a great impact on my thought process. Ravi- my dad's commitment and his command on work mesmerize's and motivate's me a lot. My every action is deeply intended to see a sparkle in their eyes. Thank you for giving me the liberty and courage to think deeper and bigger. Thank you for creating a beautiful environment Around me,

I am thankful to Umesh Chandra and Meghana for editing. Your incredible inputs gave a matt finishing to my story. Thank you Poojitha, Lasya, and Aparna for being critics of my writings, and also thankful to my friend shivamani.

A special mention to Dir. Ram Gopal Varma for motivating me with his intriguing thought-provoking speeches, movies, and interviews. I am thankful for my near and dear ones for gossiping with me and enhancing my imagination skills.

Last but not least...

Dear Readers,

My whole intention behind writing this book is all to make you happy & to see that small smile when you nostalgically connect to any part of my story. Big thanks for choosing the book and I promise you some cherishing moments with it.

ABOUT THE AUTHOR

Abhay Ramagiri is a fun-loving 18 years old undergraduate from Anurag university. His parents, Shailaja and Ravi been his friends and biggest supporters. Their interest in his ideas makes him explore more. Shrenitha (younger sister) always remains as his lovely jerry. Friends have a profound role in his life. The streets of Ramanthapur and Amberpet are the labels of his sweet memories. His day is incomplete without music and cycling.

He strongly believes that being unique differentiates the most successful person from a successful person. AROUND YOU is his first title. The urge to watch people's extreme emotions drives him to tell more and more stories. It inspired him to become an author, and he is on his way to imposing his impact on readers.

You can reach him at
abhayramagiri124@gmail.com